CLASS ASSEMBLIES

Ready-to-use ... 'or whole- ...mances

3

Veronica Clark
Kaye Umansky
Pippa Goodhart
Jenny McLachlan

Contents

Introduction 3-4

Going for Goals 5-18
Script 6-15
Teaching Notes 16-18

Robin Hood 19-34
Script 20-31
Teaching Notes 32-34

Operation Bully 35-44
Script 36-42
Teaching Notes 43-44

Year of the Rat 45-55
Script 46-52
Teaching Notes 53-55

Stage Plans 56-57
SEAL Links 58

Melody Lines 59-63

Performance licence information 64
About the authors 64
Acknowledgements 64

Introduction

Class Assemblies 3 contains everything you need to put on a successful class performance; perfect for whole-class assemblies or an end of term production for a wider audience.

The book contains:
- scripts/stories
- curriculum-based activities
- links to SEAL and literacy units
- performance tips
- melody lines for the songs

The CD contains:
- sung performances and backing tracks to sing along with
- incidental music to use in your performance (including entry and exit music for each assembly)

Whatever your resources, and whether you are aiming for something large scale, or simple and basic, this book will help you to stage a successful performance. The title page of each story provides a quick overview of the cast, story, theme and songs, and the performance notes and stage plans supply further ideas for rehearsing and staging the assembly stories.

The assemblies aim to be as flexible as possible. Although the four plays are designed for a specific age group, they can be adapted for use with other age groups.

You could present the plays as stories for use in the classroom to prompt discussion. The *Literacy Links* boxes show where you could incorporate the stories into literacy work. Each play is based around a simple moral or message, which is explored in the PSHE notes in the *Curriculum Links* section and outlined on the title page.

Preparing for the assembly

Familiarise the children with the play by reading it through a couple of times, like a story, and then discuss it with the class (see PSHE notes and *SEAL Links*). Work through some of the activities in the *Curriculum Links*. Involve the children in collecting and making props and costumes.

Take the opportunity to introduce children to new vocabulary, for example, **cast**, **props**, **scenery**, **scripts**.

Casting

Numbers for various parts are approximate, and are based on an average class size of 30. Adapt to suit your class. Some of the parts involve the children remembering lines. Make sure that the children are familiar with the cues to their lines in the narration, and encourage them to project their voices and avoid turning away from the audience when they are speaking or singing. Discuss the characters the children are playing and help them to give a convincing performance. If children have trouble remembering their lines, consider attaching their text to a prop, or incorporate some of the lines into the narration.

Staging and performance tips

Adapt these to suit your needs. You can ignore, embellish, adapt or simplify them.

Stage directions such as **stage back left** or **stage front right** are interpreted by imagining you are standing on the stage facing the audience (see also *Stage Plans*).

The stage plans show starting positions, where to put props and scenery, and the movement around the stage area.

Venue and acting space

The notes assume the plays are being performed in a large room, such as a hall. Adapt to your circumstances.

The word **stage** refers to the main performance area. This can either be a designated area of floor space or a raised stage. Teachers using a raised stage will need between one and three sets of steps for movement on and off the stage.

References to **off stage** and **below the stage** describe space outside the main performance area. Where a raised stage is being used, they refer to activity at floor level.

The stage plans

The stage plans at the back of the book are drawn on squared backgrounds. Each square represents one square metre. Adapt the plans to suit your needs.

It may sometimes be helpful to use tape or chalk to show children where to stand and the routes they take.

Costumes

Costume suggestions are given in the performance notes. For a smaller-scale production, simplify the costumes, or consider using only one element, eg, headdresses. Adding noses, whiskers, spots, etc, using face paints, can add an exciting dimension to performances.

Narrators

Adults can perform all the narration, or, as indicated in some of the scripts, the narrator's part can be split between children. Make sure the narrators are visible by standing them on stage blocks or PE benches. Spoken lines written for individual children can be incorporated into the narrator's part. If possible, use microphones for narrators. Consider giving them something special to wear, even if it's only best clothes, or bow ties and shirts.

Songs and chants

The songs in this pack are catchy and easy to learn: some consist of new words to well-known tunes, and some are simple original songs.

Sound effects

A group of children could be chosen to make any necessary sound effects. If you do so, reduce the number of cast members without speaking parts.

4

Going for Goals by Pippa Goodhart

Cast

Narrators (7) – one for each scene
Mrs Stratton, head teacher
Miss Smith, class teacher (child or adult)
Leila
Malcolm
Janey
Billy
Rest of the class (about 17)

The named children all have small speaking parts. The actor playing the part of Miss Smith has a lot to say – she could have the script attached to her clipboard. Teachers may want to customise the play by changing the names and gender of the cast to match those of people in their school.

Assembly theme

Going for Goals is concerned with recognising personal worries, identifying strategies and setting goals to overcome them, and making the effort to meet these goals. There is also a strong message about the need for children to support fellow pupils who are trying to meet goals.

Story

In assembly, the head teacher announces a Fun Sports Day. Most of the pupils are excited at the prospect, but Miss Smith and three members of her class are worried. Miss Smith is a poor timekeeper and she doubts she will remember to time the races. Leila, Malcolm and Janey all have their own worries, but Miss Smith encourages them to take part in the races. She sets achievable goals for each of them to reach.

Billy has no worries: he is confident that he can outrun everyone else. But, in the sprint relay, Billy trips over. His attitude makes it difficult for him to cope with failure and accept help. However, with a lot of encouragement from his teacher and classmates, he manages to limp over the finishing line. Miss Smith almost manages to meet her goal, but, in her concern for Billy's, she forgets to time the last race. Her pupils are quick to acknowledge that their teacher's concern for them is more important than timing the race.

Setting

The setting is a school.

Songs and chants

There are two chants and two songs (one of which has an original tune). The first chant is repeated, with variations describing the personal goals of each of the key characters.

Script: Going for Goals

Scene 1: A surprise announcement

NARRATOR 1
At the end of morning assembly, the headteacher, Mrs Stratton, made a surprise announcement.

MRS STRATTON
I've got some exciting news for you. On Friday, we are going to have a Fun Sports Day!

ALL CHILDREN
Oooooh!

CHILD 1
(ACTION – PUTS HAND UP.)
Please, Mrs Stratton, what's a Fun Sports Day?

MRS STRATTON
It's a sports day where the races are a bit like party games.

ALL CHILDREN
Hooray!

MRS STRATTON
But although the races are fun, they are still races, and the fastest team will win. Your teachers will be timing you all. Now go back to your classrooms and start practising.

(ACTION – MISS SMITH LEADS HER CLASS FROM THE HALL BACK TO THE CLASSROOM. SHE LOOKS WORRIED.)

Scene 2: Miss Smith's goal

NARRATOR 2
But not all the children in Miss Smith's class thought the Fun Sports Day was going to be fun for them. Even Miss Smith was worried.

Perhaps I shouldn't tell you this about a teacher, but, you see, even

though Miss Smith was clever and kind and good at almost everything, there was one thing that she was not at all good at: Miss Smith was not very good at keeping track of the time.

Miss Smith had a watch, and it was a fine watch, but she often forgot to look at that watch.

CD 2/12

SONG: **TICK, TOCK, TICK** *(Original)*

Miss Smith had a watch
That she hardly ever used,
So she didn't know the time or the date.

Miss Smith had a watch
That she hardly ever used,
So she kept missing things and being late.

Lessons went on too long,
Tick, tock, tick, tock.
Teacher got it all wrong,
Tick, tock, tick!

Miss Smith had a watch
That she hardly ever used,
So she kept missing things and being late.

Forward to next track

NARRATOR 2
The trouble was that Miss Smith was so enthusiastic about maths or history or art, that she completely forgot to look at her watch and to notice that it was play time, or home time, or assembly time.

MISS SMITH
Did you know that in Anglo-Saxon times, if you stole something, you could have your nose cut off as punishment?

CHILDREN
Really?!

CHILD 2
(ACTION – TUGGING AT TEACHER'S SLEEVE AND POINTING OUTSIDE.)
Please, Miss Smith, everyone's out in the playground – except us!

MISS SMITH
Oh, goodness, so they are! Sorry, children.

NARRATOR 2
In the normal run of things, the children going out to play a little bit late now and then didn't really matter. But Miss Smith knew that timing the races for her class at the Fun Sports Day really *would* matter.

MISS SMITH
Oh dear, I must make sure that I remember to use my stopwatch to time each race. If I forget, I'll really let the children down.

Forward to next track

CHANT: MY GOAL (*Original*)

Remember to time the games,
Remember to time the games,
That's what I am going to do,
Remember to time the games.

NARRATOR 2
So Miss Smith had her own private goal for sports day.

MISS SMITH
Remember to time the games.

NARRATOR 2
And some of the children in her class had their own private worries too.

Scene 3: Leila's goal

MISS SMITH
(ACTION – LOOKS AT CLIP-BOARD.)
I need to put you into four teams.

All of you children will be in the egg and spoon relay team.
(ACTION – NAMES THE CHILDREN IN THE EGG AND SPOON RELAY TEAM.)

NARRATOR 3
So the egg and spoon relay team had a practice run.
(ACTION – EGG AND SPOON RELAY TEAM LINES UP.)

ALL
Ready, steady, go!

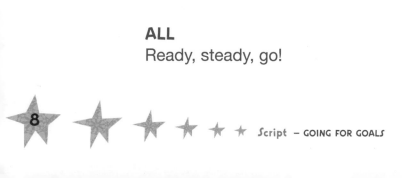

(ACTION – THE FIRST TWO CHILDREN MANAGE TO KEEP THEIR EGGS ON THEIR SPOONS, BUT LEILA, WHO IS THE THIRD TO RUN, KEEPS DROPPING HERS. THE CHILDREN IN HER TEAM CHEER AND SHOUT ENCOURAGEMENT.)

LEILA
Oh no! I'm really slow, and I keep dropping the egg! I know I'll make us lose the race!

NARRATOR 3
But Miss Smith was a kind teacher, and a good teacher. She knew how to help Leila.

MISS SMITH
Just watch the egg in the spoon and take one step at a time, Leila. I'm sure you'll do very well.

 CHANT: **MY GOAL** (*Original*)

Take one step at a time,
Take one step at a time,
That's what I am going to do,
Take one step at a time.

Forward to next track

NARRATOR 3
So Leila had her own private goal for sports day.

LEILA
Take one step at a time.
(ACTION – EGG AND SPOON RELAY TEAM SIT DOWN.)

Scene 4: Malcolm's goal

NARRATOR 4
Then Miss Smith chose children to be in the balloon relay team.

MISS SMITH
(ACTION – NAMES THE CHILDREN IN THE BALLOON RELAY TEAM.)
You are the balloon relay team. Shall we give it a go?

(ACTION – BALLOON RELAY TEAM LINES UP.)

ALL
Ready, steady, go!

(ACTION – EVERYONE MANAGES TO KEEP THE BALLOON MOVING ABOVE THEIR HEADS, EXCEPT FOR MALCOLM, WHO DOESN'T CONCENTRATE. HIS TEAM GET ANNOYED WITH HIM.)

MALCOLM
Oh no! I just can't concentrate! I know I'll make us lose the race!

NARRATOR 4
But Miss Smith was a kind teacher. She knew how to help Malcolm.

MISS SMITH
Just concentrate on passing the balloon, and keep your mind on the game, Malcolm. I'm sure you'll do very well.

Forward to next track

CHANT: MY GOAL (*Original*)

Keep my mind on the game,
Keep my mind on the game,
That's what I am going to do,
Keep my mind on the game.

NARRATOR 4
So Malcolm had his own private goal for sports day.

MALCOLM
Keep my mind on the game.
(ACTION – BALLOON TEAM SITS DOWN.)

Scene 5: Janey's goal

NARRATOR 5
The dressing-up relay team members were chosen next.

MISS SMITH
(ACTION – NAMES THE CHILDREN IN THE DRESSING UP RELAY TEAM.)
You are the dressing-up relay team. Shall we do a practice run?

(ACTION – DRESSING UP RELAY TEAM LINES UP.)

ALL
Ready, steady, go!

(ACTION – THE FIRST TWO CHILDREN RUN TO THE BOX, PICK UP AND PUT ON HATS, SCARVES AND BAGS AND RUN TO THE BACK OF THEIR LINES. THEN IT'S JANEY'S TURN. SHE HOVERS AROUND THE BOX, UNABLE TO

DECIDE WHAT TO WEAR. THE CHILDREN IN HER TEAM URGE HER TO HURRY UP. SHE PUTS ON A HAT AND EVERYONE LAUGHS – BUT NOT IN AN UNKIND WAY. JANEY THROWS THE HAT ON THE FLOOR AND LOOKS AS THOUGH SHE'S GOING TO CRY.)

JANEY

I can't decide what to choose, and I don't like people laughing at me. I know I'm going to make us lose the race.

NARRATOR 5

But Miss Smith was a kind teacher. She knew how to help Janey.

MISS SMITH

They'll be laughing *with* you, not at you, Janey. Just relax and have fun. I'm sure you'll do very well.

CD 6/16

CHANT: MY GOAL *(Original)*

Just relax and have fun,
Just relax and have fun,
That's what I am going to do,
Just relax and have fun.

Forward to next track

NARRATOR 5

So Janey had her own private goal for sports day.

JANEY

Just relax and have fun!

CD 7/17

CHANT: GIVE IT A GO! *(Original)*

(CHILDREN) Give it a go! Give it a go!
(LEILA) But when I'm running, I'm so slow!
(MALCOLM) And I'll go and drop the balloon — oh no!
(JANEY) Dressing in public? I don't think so!
(MISS SMITH) Can I get the timing? I just don't know!
(ALL) We're all of us full of worries and woe.

(BILLY, JUMPING FORWARD TO ANNOUNCE HIMSELF)
... except for me! I'm Billy!

Forward to next track

Scene 6: The big day arrives

NARRATOR 6

At last, it was Friday. Leila, Malcolm and Janey were quite nervous. So was Miss Smith. Everyone was excited, but Billy was the most excited of all. He was a fast runner, and had been chosen for the sprint relay.

BILLY

My team will win, just wait and see!
Nobody else is as fast as me.

I'll win for our team all on my own!

(ACTION – EVERYONE ROLLS THEIR EYES AND TURNS AWAY.)

SONG: SILLY BILLY (Here we go gathering nuts in May)

Billy says he's going to win the race,
Win the race, win the race.
Billy says he's going to win the race,
Without the help of his friends.

NARRATOR 6

The first race was the egg and spoon relay. The children lined up.
Miss Smith held her stopwatch ready.
(ACTION – EGG AND SPOON RELAY TEAM LINE UP AS BEFORE.)

MISS SMITH

Good luck, all of you!

CHILDREN

We'll cheer for you,
We're here for you –
Ready, steady, go!

(SOUND EFFECT AND ACTION – A QUIET, REGULAR TAPPING ON A WOODBLOCK INDICATES THAT MISS SMITH IS TIMING THE RACE. LEILA MANAGES TO KEEP THE EGG ON HER SPOON, AND FINISHES WITH A BIG GRIN. AT THE END OF THE RACE, EVERYONE CHEERS.)

CHILDREN

Hooray for Leila!

LEILA
I'm so pleased I reached my goal,
Come on class, we're on a roll!

NARRATOR 6
Next, it was time for the balloon relay race. The children lined up.
Miss Smith held her stopwatch ready.
(ACTION – BALLOON RELAY TEAM LINES UP AS BEFORE.)

MISS SMITH
Good luck, all of you!

CHILDREN
We'll cheer for you,
We're here for you –
Ready, steady, go!

(SOUND EFFECT AND ACTION – QUIET, REGULAR TAPPING ON A
WOODBLOCK INDICATES THAT MISS SMITH IS TIMING THE RACE.
MALCOLM MANAGES TO CONCENTRATE FOR THE WHOLE RACE. AT THE
END OF THE RACE, EVERYONE CHEERS.)

CHILDREN
Hooray for Malcolm!

MALCOLM
I'm so pleased I reached my goal,
Come on class, we're on a roll!

NARRATOR 6
The third race was the dressing-up relay.
(ACTION – DRESSING UP RELAY TEAM LINES UP AS BEFORE.)

MISS SMITH
Good luck, all of you!

CHILDREN
We'll cheer for you,
We're here for you –
Ready, steady, go!

(SOUND EFFECT AND ACTION – A QUIET, REGULAR TAPPING ON A
WOODBLOCK INDICATES THAT MISS SMITH IS TIMING THE RACE.

WHEN IT'S JANEY'S TURN TO RUN TO THE DRESSING UP BOX, SHE TAKES
A DEEP BREATH AND GETS ON WITH IT. AT THE END OF THE RACE, EVERYONE
CHEERS.)

CHILDREN
Hooray for Janey!

JANEY
I'm so pleased I reached my goal,
Come on class, we're on a roll!

Scene 7: Billy

NARRATOR 7
Finally, it was time for the relay sprint.

(ACTION – THE RUNNERS LINE UP. BILLY IS THIRD IN LINE. HE CAN HARDLY
CONTAIN HIMSELF. MISS SMITH HAS HER STOPWATCH AT THE READY.)

CHILDREN
We'll cheer for you,
We're here for you –
Ready, steady, go!

BILLY
Huh! I don't need help from anyone. Just you watch me go!

(ACTION – THE RACE STARTS. THE WOODBLOCK SOUNDS. WHEN IT'S BILLY'S
TURN, HE SETS OFF AT TOP SPEED, BUT FALLS OVER WITHIN THE FIRST FEW
METRES. HE TRIES TO GET UP, BUT CAN'T. MISS SMITH STOPS TIMING THE
RACE – THE WOODBLOCK STOPS TOO – AND RUNS OVER TO HIM.)

MISS SMITH
Oh, Billy! Are you ok? Do you want help?

BILLY
(LOOKS EMBARRASSED.)
I don't need any help! What's the point? We can't win now!

MISS SMITH
Winning doesn't matter Billy. The most important thing is taking part
and finishing the race! Come on – we'll help you!

BILLY
I don't need … er. Yes, please, I think I *do* need help …

NARRATOR 7

So the children helped Billy to limp over the line.

(ACTION – BILLY'S TEAM HELP HIM TO FINISH. THE RACE CONTINUES, WITHOUT THE WOODBLOCK. BILLY MANAGES A SMILE AND SHAKES HANDS WITH HIS TEAM AS THEY FINISH THE RACE. EVERYONE CHEERS.)

CHILDREN
Hooray for Billy!

 SONG: SENSIBLE BILLY *(Here we go gathering nuts in May)*

Forward to next track

Billy got up and he finished the race,
Finished the race, finished the race.
Billy got up and he finished the race,
With just a bit of help.

NARRATOR 7

So, with the help of their friends, Leila, Malcolm and Janey had achieved their goals. And Billy? He'd learnt something important. He'd learnt not to be so boastful. And he'd learnt that he did need to accept help from his friends after all. But what about Miss Smith? Had she achieved her goal?

MISS SMITH
(ACTION – HOLDS UP THE WATCH, LOOKING HORRIFIED.)
Oh, no! I forgot to finish timing the last race!

CHILDREN

That's because you were looking after us! Thank you, Miss Smith!

NARRATOR 7

Poor Miss Smith. She had been so busy making sure Billy was all right that she stopped timing the last race. But her pupils didn't mind. They knew that Miss Smith was a good teacher because she really cared about them, and that's the most important thing of all.

 CHANT: WE GAVE IT A GO! *(Original)*

We gave it a go! We gave it a go!
We set our goals and didn't say no.
We did our best and put on a show.
Working together worked best, you know!
Going for goals can help us grow,
Away from all our worries and woe!

Performance Notes

Staging and performance tips (see stage plan)

- After the first scene, there is no movement on and off the main staging area. In scenes 2 to 7, the children sit in a class group in the back third of the stage. The front two thirds of the stage are used for the races.

- **Scene 1:** the children pretend to be in a school assembly. They sit, with Miss Smith, facing the head teacher, who stands over on the left. Assembly over, Miss Smith leads her pupils off the stage on the left, around in front of the stage and back onstage at the back on the right. This time, the children sit in two rows, facing the audience.

- **Scene 2:** choose one of the pupils to add a quiet, woodblock accompaniment for the third stanza of *Tick, Tock, Tick*.

- **Scenes 3, 4 and 5:** these scenes cover the practice egg and spoon, balloon and dressing-up races. Not everyone in the three teams has a turn in these preliminary race scenes, but on Fun Sports Day (Scenes 6 and 7) all four races are completed, and all the children participate.

- Before each trial run, Miss Smith looks at her clipboard and reads out the names of the children in the team. With the exception of the dressing up race (which will take too long if you have more than four children taking part), teams should comprise five or six children. The children line up on the right of the stage for their races, facing towards the left. Leila, Malcolm and Janey stand third in their team lines. Miss Smith stands on the left – the children run towards her and back again.

- The races are all relays. In the egg and spoon race, for example, the first child runs to the other side of the stage and back, then hands the egg and spoon to the second child. The second child does the same and hands the equipment to Leila. Leila runs slowly across the stage but keeps dropping her egg. The race rehearsal stops at this point.

- The balloon race team stands well spaced out. The child at the front holds a balloon. This is passed backwards over the children's heads until it reaches the person at the end of the line. He or she runs to the front with the balloon, and the sequence starts again. Stop the race after two or three runs when the children are showing annoyance at Malcolm's lack of concentration.

- In the dressing up relay race, two children have a turn before Janey runs to the box of clothes.

- **Scene 6:** in this scene, all three races are completed and all three children meet their goals. Miss Smith remembers to time the races, as is indicated by the quiet, regular tapping on a woodblock that accompanies each race.

- **Scene 7:** Billy stands third in his team line. He runs to the other end of the stage, but trips on his way back. Miss Smith stops timing the race (the woodblock taps stop too), and picks him up. Billy is helped back to his team and the race continues.

Scenery

- Place one or two freestanding display boards at the back of the stage. Cover the boards with schoolwork related, if possible, to the theme of the play.

Props

- Miss Smith needs a wristwatch, clipboard, pen and stopwatch.
- For the races you need an egg and spoon, a balloon, and as many hats, scarves and bags as you have children in the dressing up race. Put the clothes in a big box.

Costumes

- The children wear PE kit. The teaching staff wear 'grown-up' clothes.

Sound effects

- Use a two-tone woodblock to accompany *Tick, tock, tick* and during the races to indicate that Miss Smith is timing them.

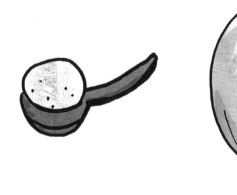

Curriculum Links

Literacy Link
Stories with familiar settings.

PSHE

- Discuss the following lines from the play:
  - Leila: 'I just know that I'll make us lose the race.'
  - Malcolm: 'I just can't concentrate.'
  - Janey: 'I just don't like people laughing at me.'
  - Billy: 'I'll win for my team all on my own.'

- Identify the problems faced by the four children. Leila thinks she's hopeless at everything and that her classmates think badly of her because of this (low self-esteem). Malcolm fools around a bit and forgets what he's meant to be doing (poor concentration). Janey thinks everyone is looking at her and laughing at her (self-consciousness). Billy thinks he's better than everyone else and boasts (over-confidence).

- Do any of the children in your class identify with the personal worries and problems experienced by Leila, Malcolm, Janey and Billy? Encourage them to talk about it – how they feel, how it makes them behave.

- Discuss how personal problems can make people miserable, get in the way of learning and, in certain situations, be annoying for other people, including teachers.

How to be a good sport

- Competitive races can be difficult for some children, especially those who expect to win and don't, and those who know they have no hope of winning. Talk about what it means to be a good sport and how you show it (even if you don't feel it).

PE

- In groups, make up new fun races using toys or PE equipment. Try the races out and choose a few that work well. Organise a Fun Sports Day that includes other classes. Write instructions for each race with accompanying diagrams, and give them to the other participants. Design and make badges or rosettes for winning teams.

Design and technology

- Make several lengths of bunting by decorating triangles or rectangles cut out of strong paper. Fold them over at one end, lay the fold over a length of string and secure with staples. Alternatively, cut flags out of coloured fabric and sew them onto tape using a sewing machine.

Robin Hood by Kaye Umansky

Cast

Narrators (4)
Robin Hood
The Merry Men: Little John, Will Scarlett, Allan A-Dale,
Much the Miller, Friar Tuck
The Sheriff of Nottingham
The Sheriff's henchmen (about 4)
Maid Marian
Marian's maids (4)
King Richard
Villagers (about 9)

Assembly theme

The main theme of *Robin Hood* is justice. The play comments on the inequalities between rich and poor, the greed of some people with power, and the unorthodox method adopted by Robin and his men to help the oppressed.

Story

King Richard is away overseas, fighting in the Crusades. Back at home, the greedy Sheriff of Nottingham takes advantage of the king's absence to embark on a get-rich-quick campaign. Assisted by his evil henchmen, he makes frequent visits to the local village to demand illegal taxes.

Robin Hood, dismayed by the plight of the villagers, gathers together a band of Merry Men. They vow to bring justice to the land, and set about robbing the rich and giving away their plunder to the poor. Maid Marian, to the disgust of her moaning maids, joins Robin in his forest hideaway.

Despite their best efforts, the Sheriff and his men are unable to catch Robin. The Sheriff's humiliation is complete when he is ambushed and relieved of his ill-gained money and fine clothes.

King Richard returns. The villagers tell him all about the evil doings of the Sheriff, who is thrown in jail. The bad times are finally over, and Robin is declared a hero.

Setting

The play, set in Norman times, switches between the village and Sherwood Forest.

Songs

Three of the four songs are set to well-known tunes.

Script: Robin Hood

Scene 1: Watch out, Sheriff!

NARRATOR 1
Lords, ladies, gentlemen, children, teachers! May we present –

ALL NARRATORS
The story of Robin Hood!

(ACTION – ENTER VILLAGERS WITH BASKETS OF FRUIT, BUNDLES OF FIREWOOD, SACKS OF FLOUR, A PIE, A BAG OF APPLES, ETC.)

 SONG: **BOLD, BRAVE ROBIN** (*I came from Alabama*)

Gonna tell you all a story,
And we hope you find it good.
It's the story of an outlaw,
With the name of Robin Hood.

(ACTION – ROBIN BOUNDS IN AND POSES WITH BOW AND ARROW.)

He lived in Sherwood Forest,
Where he built a secret den.
And he had some bold adventures,
With his band of Merry Men.

Bold, brave Robin!
We'd like to shake your hand.
Three cheers for noble Robin,
Who brought justice to the land.

ROBIN
That's me, folks!

VILLAGERS
Hooray! Good old Robin! You're our hero!

(ACTION – VILLAGERS SHAKE HIS HAND AND CLAP HIM ON THE BACK.)

 Forward to next track

VILLAGER 1

Hold it! Stop a minute. We should begin at the beginning.

(ACTION – VILLAGERS NOD. ROBIN BOUNDS OFF. IMMEDIATELY THERE IS A MOOD CHANGE. THE VILLAGERS SIGH AND LOOK DEJECTED.)

MUSIC: SAD MUSIC (*Original*)

NARRATOR 2

Times were troubled in Sherwood. King Richard was away over the seas, fighting in the crusades.
(SOUND EFFECT – DISTANT THUNDER.)

England was in chaos.

NARRATOR 3

The poor people had the worst of it.

VILLAGERS

As usual!

NARRATOR 4

They had to pay taxes to the cruel Sheriff of Nottingham.

(ACTION – ENTER THE SHERIFF WITH HIS HENCHMEN.)

VILLAGERS

BOOOOOO! SSSSSSSSS!

SHERIFF

That's enough of that! Turn out your pockets. It's tax day!

VILLAGERS

What? Again?!

SHERIFF

That's right. That way I get very, very rich.
(TO HENCHMEN.)
Well, don't just stand there!

(ACTION – HENCHMEN ROB VILLAGERS WITH MUCH PUSHING AND SWORD WAVING, THEN RETURN TO THEIR PLACES IN THE MIDDLE OF THE STAGE.)

VILLAGER 2 (TO AUDIENCE.)

This is the perfect place for a sad song.

SONG: SO BAD (*My bonny lies over the ocean*)

The Sheriff is nasty and greedy,
He fills all our hearts with dismay.
He taxes the poor and the needy,
And takes all our money away.

So bad, so sad,
To take all our money away, away.
So bad, so sad,
To take all our money away.

Forward to next track

(ACTION – ALL VILLAGERS SIGH.)

VILLAGER 3
This is so unfair.

SHERIFF
Hah! As if I care!

(ACTION – EXIT SHERIFF AND HENCHMEN, LAUGHING AND CRUNCHING
STOLEN APPLES. ENTER ROBIN, BOUNDING.)

ROBIN
I saw that! Let's give him another boo!

ALL
BOOOOOOO!

(ACTION – ENCOURAGE AUDIENCE TO JOIN IN.)

VILLAGERS
It's so unfair! It's so unfair!
To rob the poor without a care!

ROBIN
I'll make him sorry, just you see.
From now on, he's my enemy!

ALL
Watch out, Sheriff!

(ACTION – EXIT ALL.)

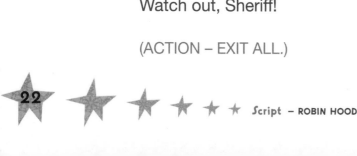

Script – ROBIN HOOD

Scene 2: Who will join me?

NARRATOR 1
Word began to spread that Robin was looking for people to help him stand up to the wicked Sheriff of Nottingham.

NARRATOR 2
He didn't have much trouble finding them.

(ACTION – ENTER ROBIN, BOUNDING.)

ROBIN (TO AUDIENCE.)
Who will join me?

(ACTION – MERRY MEN ENTER AND LINE UP ACROSS THE STAGE.)

MERRY MEN
We will!

(ACTION – THE MERRY MEN POINT TO THEIR NAMES AS THEY INTRODUCE THEMSELVES.)

LITTLE JOHN
I'm Little John, the big one!

WILL SCARLETT
I'm Will Scarlett, the red one!

ALLAN A-DALE
I'm Allan A-Dale, the musical one, tra-la!

MUCH THE MILLER
I'm Much the Miller! No-one knows *much* about me. Get it?

(ACTION – ALL GROAN.)

FRIAR TUCK
I'm Friar Tuck, the priest!

MERRY MEN
And together, we're the Merry Men!

Forward to
next track

SONG: WE´RE THE MERRY MEN! *(Knees up Mother Brown)*

We´re the Merry Men, the very Merry Men,
We laugh and sing like anything,
`Cos we´re the Merry Men!

We live in the wood, helping Robin Hood,
We hang out in our secret den,
`Cos we´re the Merry Men!

NARRATOR 3
Robin was very pleased with his bold, brave men.

NARRATOR 4
But it was time to get serious.

NARRATOR 1
Time to talk about big, important things.

NARRATOR 2
Things like freedom, and justice for the poor.

(ACTION – ROBIN AND THE MEN GET INTO A HUDDLE AND MUTTER.)

NARRATOR 3
It didn't take them long to come up with ideas.

(ACTION – THE MEN GET BACK INTO THEIR LINE.)

LITTLE JOHN
We must stop the Sheriff stealing from the poor.

WILL SCARLETT
The rich have too much and the poor have nothing!

ALLAN A-DALE
Fair taxes for everyone!

MUCH THE MILLER
Justice for the people!

FRIAR TUCK
And free ice cream!

 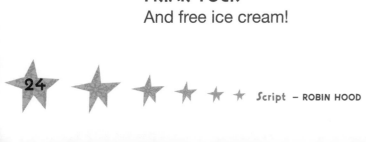 *Script* – ROBIN HOOD

NARRATOR 4

They talked all night. When the sun rose, they knew what they had to do.

(ACTION – EXIT ROBIN AND MEN.)

Scene 3: Maid Marian

NARRATOR 1

Maid Marian lived in a big castle with her daddy.

NARRATOR 2

She often played in the forest, and was secret friends with Robin.

NARRATOR 3

But she didn't have any Merry Men.

NARRATOR 4

All she had were Moaning Maids.

(ACTION – ENTER MARIAN AND HER MAIDS.)

MARIAN

Come on, everyone, let's play hide and seek.

MAID 1

This is not right, this is not good.

MAID 2

We must not play out in the wood.

MAID 3

The wood is where the outlaws roam.

MAID 4

You'll get told off when you go home.

ALL

We're telling!

MARIAN

Rubbish. You hide and I'll count to ten.

(ACTION – MAIDS HIDE BEHIND THE TREES. MARIAN HIDES HER EYES.)

MARIAN
One … two … three …

ROBIN (OFF STAGE.)
Marian! Come and see the den!

MARIAN
Coming!

(ACTION – MARIAN RUNS OFF. MAIDS RUN BACK INTO THE MIDDLE, SCREAMING.)

MAID 1
This is not right, this is not good!

MAID 2
She's gone to play with Robin Hood!

MAID 3
That's very naughty! Really bad!

MAID 4
Let's run back home and find her dad.

ALL
We're telling!

(ACTION – EXIT MAIDS, NOSES IN THE AIR.)

Scene 4: Justice For All!

(ACTION – THE MERRY MEN LOUNGE AROUND WITH BAGS OF GOLD. FRIAR TUCK HAS A STOLEN CAKE. ENTER ROBIN AND MARIAN.)

ROBIN (TO MARIAN.)
Here's the den and they're my men.

(ACTION – THE MERRY MEN JUMP UP AND REPEAT *WE'RE THE MERRY MEN*.)

REPEAT SONG: WE'RE THE MERRY MEN!

We're the Merry Men, the very Merry Men …

Forward to
next track

LITTLE JOHN
It's a good haul today, Robin!

WILL SCARLETT
We held up a coach.

ALLAN A-DALE
Three bags of gold, look!

MUCH THE MILLER
You should have heard 'em complaining!

FRIAR TUCK
Who's that? (ACTION – POINTS AT MARIAN.)

ROBIN
This is Marian.

MARIAN
Hello.

MERRY MEN
A girl?

ROBIN
Yes. She's joining the gang. Problems?

(ACTION – THE MEN HUDDLE TOGETHER, MUTTERING, THEN REACH A DECISION.)

LITTLE JOHN
Come on, boys. Bow to the lady.

(ACTION – THE MERRY MEN BOW.)

MARIAN
Did you steal all that money?

WILL SCARLETT
We don't call it stealing.

ALLAN A-DALE
We only rob the rich.

MUCH THE MILLER
Then we give it back to the poor.

FRIAR TUCK
That's what we call justice!

SONG: JUSTICE FOR ALL (Original)

The rich need to share
The things they have got.
The poor have too little,
The rich have a lot.
One law for the rich,
And one for the poor,
There's got to be Justice For All!

Justice For All, Justice For All,
The poor and the weak,
The meek and the small.
Justice For All, Justice For All,
There's got to be Justice For All!

Forward to next track

(ACTION – EXIT ALL.)

Scene 5: I'll get him!

NARRATOR 1
Meanwhile, the Sheriff of Nottingham was fuming.

SHERIFF (OFF STAGE.)
GRRRRR!

NARRATOR 2
He sent out his soldiers again and again to find Robin and his band – but with no luck.

NARRATOR 3
As the weeks went by, he got angrier and angrier.

SHERIFF (OFF STAGE.)
GRRRRRRRRR!

NARRATOR 4
So, to take his mind off things, he decided to go to the village and seize yet more taxes.

NARRATOR 1
The way home was through the forest.

NARRATOR 2
It was a great pity that he was wearing his best coat and new boots ...

 Script – ROBIN HOOD

(ACTION – ENTER SHERIFF AND HENCHMEN WITH BAGS OF MONEY AND A STOLEN PIE.)

SHERIFF
Hah! That was worth doing! More money for me!

ROBIN (OFF STAGE.)
Hold it right there!

(ACTION – ROBIN BOUNDS ON WITH HIS MEN. THEY BRISTLE WITH WEAPONS.)

SHERIFF
It's him! Get him, men!

LITTLE JOHN
I wouldn't if I were you.

(ACTION – THE MERRY MEN CONFRONT THE SHERIFF AND HENCHMEN.)

WILL SCARLETT
Drop your weapons!

ALLAN A-DALE
We'll take that! (ACTION – TAKES BAG OF MONEY.)

MUCH THE MILLER
And this! (ACTION – TAKES ANOTHER BAG OF MONEY.)

FRIAR TUCK
And this! (ACTION – TAKES THE PIE.)

ROBIN
That's a very smart coat you're wearing, Sheriff. Nice boots too.

LITTLE JOHN
Take 'em off! (ACTION – MOVES OVER TO THE SHERIFF.)

SHERIFF
How dare you!

WILL SCARLETT
Don't make me see red! (ACTION – WAVES DAGGER.)

NARRATOR 3
And the sheriff was forced to remove his fine clothes and hand them over.

(ACTION – THE SHERIFF TAKES OFF HIS COAT AND BOOTS, AND HANDS THEM TO LITTLE JOHN AND ALLAN A-DALE.)

NARRATOR 4
He didn't like that one bit.

ALLAN A-DALE
Off you go, cheerio!

MUCH THE MILLER
See you, toodleoo!

FRIAR TUCK
Bye-bye, thanks for the pie!

(ACTION – EXIT THE SHERIFF AND HENCHMEN, TO LAUGHTER.)

SHERIFF (AS HE EXITS.)
I'll get you, Hood! Just see if I don't! (ACTION – SHAKES FIST.)

(ACTION – EXIT ROBIN AND MEN.)

Scene 6: Long live the king!

NARRATOR 1
He tried. Oh, how the sheriff tried.

NARRATOR 2
But despite his best efforts, he never did manage to outwit Robin.

NARRATOR 3
And at long last – there was wonderful news! King Richard came back from the wars!

(ACTION – ENTER MARIAN'S MAIDS AND THE VILLAGERS, WAVING FLAGS.)

ALL
Long live the king! Hooray for Richard!

(ACTION – ENTER KING RICHARD, GRACIOUSLY WAVING. EVERYONE CHEERS.)

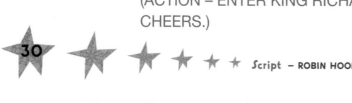

NARRATOR 4

At long last, Robin could stop being an outlaw and live a normal life.

NARRATOR 1

When King Richard heard about the wicked things that the Sheriff of Nottingham had done, he was really angry.

NARRATOR 2

He ordered him and his henchmen to be clapped in jail.

(ACTION – ENTER THE SHERIFF AND HIS HENCHMEN, IN CHAINS, ACCOMPANIED BY TWO OF THE BURLIER VILLAGERS.)

ALL

BOOOOOO!

SHERIFF

GRRRRRR!

(ACTION – EXIT THE SHERIFF AND HIS HENCHMEN.)

NARRATOR 3

The bad times were finally over.

NARRATOR 4

Justice returned to the land.

(ACTION – ENTER ROBIN, MARIAN AND THE MERRY MEN.)

ALL

Hooray! It's Robin!

(ACTION – ROBIN KNEELS IN FRONT OF THE KING, WHO RAISES HIM AND SHAKES HIS HAND. EVERYONE CHEERS AGAIN.)

 REPEAT SONG: BOLD, BRAVE ROBIN

 Gonna tell you all a story ...

Performance Notes

Staging and performance tips (see stage plan)

- There are three main entry points: villagers enter and leave from the right, Robin and his men from the left, Marian, her maids and King Richard from the back. The villagers keep to the right of the stage, and the outlaws mainly keep to the forest, on the left. The Sheriff and his henchmen enter from the front in scenes 1 and 6, but in scene 5 they use the same entry point as the villagers.

- **Scene 1:** the Sheriff and his henchmen (in pairs) march down the centre of the hall, between the audience, and onto the stage, centre front. The henchmen turn to face the audience. They break ranks to rob the villagers, then march off the same way and sit on the floor until their next appearance.

- **Scene 2:** Robin and his new recruits all enter from the left and line up across the front of the stage. The Merry Men always speak in the same order – it will help them to remember their lines if they stand in the order in which they speak.

- **Scene 3:** Marian and her maids enter centre back. Marian comes to the front of the stage to count while the maids hide behind the trees. When Robin calls to Marian, she runs off through the forest on the left. The maids come out of hiding, hastily move back to the safety of the middle, have one last moan, then flounce off at the back.

- **Scene 4:** the Merry Men stand in a semi-circle holding their gold. Robin and Marian enter centre back and stand at the front in the middle for the rest of the scene. Everyone exits stage left.

- **Scene 5:** the Sheriff and his henchmen enter stage right. Led by the Sheriff, they march towards the forest but are stopped in the middle of the stage by Robin's men. In the tussle that follows, the henchmen are bundled over to the right of the stage and surrounded. Robin and the Sheriff confront each other centre stage. Little John and Allan A-Dale relieve the Sheriff of his fine clothes.

- **Scene 6:** Robin, Marian and the Merry Men enter stage left. During the final song, which everyone joins in with, Robin kneels in front of King Richard. The king helps Robin to his feet and shakes his hand.

☀ Scenery

- Make four freestanding trees. To make the trunks, roll up and secure metre-high lengths of corrugated card, and paint brown. Cut large, cauliflower shaped treetops out of strong card, paint branches on them, and cover with tissue paper leaves in various shades of green. Staple the treetops firmly to the the trunks, then support the trees on rounders hurdles.

☀ Props

- **Name labels:** all characters have their names written large on labels, which they wear somewhere about their dress – on their hats, on something they always carry, or hung about their necks, eg, POOR VILLAGER, MILKMAID, MARIAN, KING RICHARD, etc. Robin's name could be picked out in green sequins.
- **Villagers:** baskets of fruit, bundles of firewood, sacks of flour, pies, chains, flags.
- **Merry Men:** bow and arrow for Robin, small guitar for Allan A-Dale (slung over his back), cake, three large bags of money (print GOLD on the front of the bags).
- **Henchmen:** swords, two large bags of money, large pie.

☀ Costumes

- **Robin Hood and his Merry Men:** green or brown trousers (except for Will Scarlett, who is in red). Leather belts, white shirts, waistcoats, and boots or plimsolls. Friar Tuck wears baggy trousers and a padded-out top under a long, brown coat or tunic, plus a hood.

- **Marian and her maids:** long skirts with long-sleeved tops or dresses in plain material. To give the effect of Norman-style sleeves, attach silky scarves to wrists. Thin plaited headbands.

- **Norman henchmen:** black trousers tucked into long black or grey socks and long-sleeved black or grey tunics with belts.

- **Sheriff and King Richard:** long-sleeved tunics in plain, rich colours. Tie cloaks over one shoulder and keep in place with brooches. The king wears a simple crown.

- **Villagers:** the women wear long skirts with blouses tucked in at the waist, and aprons or shawls. The men wear trousers with shirts hanging out, belts over the shirts, and bare feet.

☀ Sound effects

- **Distant thunder:** drum roll using soft beaters.

Curriculum Links

PSHE

- Robin Hood and his men robbed the rich and gave the stolen goods to the poor. Do the children think it was acceptable for Robin to steal in these circumstances? Was there any other way he could have helped the poor?

- The Merry Men talk about 'big, important things. Things like freedom, and justice for the poor.' What did they mean by 'justice for the poor'?

- Do the children think anything in school is unfair? Discuss their answers. Which issues are important to the children? What can be done about them? To whom should complaints be put? Who could represent the pupils?

- If people living in Britain think things are unfair and that change is needed, what can they do about it? (Speak to their Member of Parliament or local councillor, write letters to a newspaper, have a petition, demonstrate.)

Taxes
- What are taxes? To whom are taxes paid? Does everyone pay the same taxes whether they are rich or poor?

- What do taxes pay for? Ask the children to look around next time they are in town and see what taxes buy (most teachers, nurses and doctors, most schools and hospitals, the fire service, the police, street lighting, drains, parks, etc).

Literacy
- There are many tales about Robin Hood. Make up stories involving Robin and no more than three other characters. The children could write the stories in comic format with pictures and speech bubbles. Let the children have a go at converting their comic stories into play format with a cast and props list and suggestions for scenery and costumes. Act out a few of the plays.

History
- Do some research into life in England in the reign of Richard I. How did the poor people live? (Where did they live, what did they wear, what work did they do, what did they eat?)

- Find out about Norman castles – perhaps there is one near your school. Talk about the castles' defences.

Operation Bully by Jenny McLachlan

Cast
Narrators (5)
Z (boss at MI5)
Agents 001, 002, 003 and 004
Mr Simms (teacher)
Reshma, Louise, Alex (literacy group)
Tom, Jack, Rahim, Beth, Harry (playground group)
Jibril, Crystal, Chloe, Megan, Elliot, Jade, Frank (lunch queue group)
Other students (about 4)

All the named characters, except Megan, have speaking parts.

Assembly theme

Operation Bully illustrates how bullying can be done in several ways, some of which are hard to spot. The play shows how students can stand up to bullies and make bullying less likely to recur.

Story

Four secret agents from MI5 are instructed by their boss (who is a bit of a bully herself) to visit a local school where there have been reports of bullying. Their mission is to track down the bullies and put a stop to their behaviour.

The agents infiltrate a literacy lesson at Southhill School, during which Reshma and Louise tease one of their classmates, a shy boy called Alex. Their bullying is so subtle that Agent 001 has difficulty spotting it.

Out in the playground Tom, Jack and Rahim are playing football. One of them wacks the ball into Agent 003, but rather than apologise, Jack and Tom attempt to intimidate her. The agents are pleased to see some of the pupils standing up to the bullies.

In the lunch queue, Jibril, Chloe and Jade are making life difficult for a few children. Crystal, Elliot and Frank all respond in a way that makes it clear they are not intimidated by the bullies' words and actions. It looks as though the school doesn't need secret agents to sort out the bullying problem after all.

Setting

The play begins and ends in MI5 headquarters in London. In between, we visit a classroom, the playground and the lunch queue at Southhill School.

Songs

There are three songs, one of which is sung to a well-known tune.

Script: Operation Bully

Scene 1: Z's office, MI5

NARRATOR
Location: MI5 headquarters, London. Time: 0800 hours.
Four of our country's best secret agents are enjoying a cup of tea and a digestive biscuit while they wait for their next top-secret mission.

(ACTION – THE FOUR AGENTS, WHO ARE WEARING RAINCOATS AND SUNGLASSES, LOUNGE ABOUT READING MAGAZINES.)

And here it comes!

(ACTION – Z WALKS INTO THE ROOM AND ALL THE AGENTS LEAP TO THEIR FEET, BRUSHING CRUMBS OFF THEIR CLOTHES AND TUCKING IN THEIR SHIRTS. THEY STAND TO ATTENTION.)

Z
Where's 007?

AGENT 001
On holiday on the Isle of Wight, Ma'am.

Z
Well, I suppose I'll have to make do with you lot then. Listen to this.

(ACTION – SHE READS FROM A DOCUMENT MARKED 'TOP SECRET'.)

'Reports are coming in that a bully has managed to infiltrate Southhill School. Several students are being hurt and it is essential for the happiness of everyone at the school that the bullying is stopped immediately. Agents must be sent undercover to discover who is responsible for the bulling, and to put an end to it. This message will self-destruct in two seconds ...' OW!

(ACTION – Z BLOWS ON FINGERS AS THE DOCUMENT 'DISAPPEARS'.)

AGENT 002
I'm not sure I'd know how to spot a bully.

AGENT 003
I think they hit and punch people.

AGENT OO4

Don't they call people names?

Z

(SIGHS.)

Alright, stop wasting time. Here are your disguises. Make sure you don't let me down!

(ACTION – Z HANDS THEM A RUCKSACK AND EXITS.)

NARRATOR

In no time at all, the intrepid secret agents put on their disguises and go undercover at Southhill School.

(ACTION – THE FOUR AGENTS STUFF THEIR OVERCOATS IN THE RUCKSACK. UNDERNEATH THEIR COATS THEY ARE WEARING SCHOOL UNIFORM. LEAVING THEIR SUNGLASSES ON, THEY HEAD TOWARDS SOUTHHILL SCHOOL, SINGING *HOW CAN WE SPOT A BULLY*. THE SCHOOL CHILDREN STAND UP AND JOIN IN.)

SONG: HOW CAN WE SPOT A BULLY? (Original)

How can we spot a bully?
How can we spot a bully?
Do they slap and kick and punch like this?
Slap and kick and punch like this?
Slap and kick and punch like this?
Let's find that bully.

How can we spot a bully?
How can we spot a bully?
Do they call you names to your face?
Call you names to your face?
Call you names to your face?
Let's find that bully.

Forward to next track

(ACTION – MR SIMMS RINGS THE BELL FOR THE END OF BREAK. THE CHILDREN TURN AND SIT DOWN FACING HIM.)

Scene 2: The classroom

NARRATOR

Location: Southhill School, Mr Simms' literacy lesson. Time: 0930 hours.

MR SIMMS
Right, I'd like you to get into groups and work on your stories.

(ACTION – THE PUPILS AND AGENTS 002, 003 AND 004 GET INTO THEIR GROUPS. RESHMA AND LOUISE'S GROUP SIT TOGETHER AT THE FRONT, FACING THE AUDIENCE. ALEX AND AGENT 001 STAND NEAR MR SIMMS, UNSURE WHERE TO GO.)

MR SIMMS
Wake up, Alex, and you too, new boy (Mr Simms points at 001). Do what I told you to do! Ask Reshma and Louise if you can work with them.

(ACTION – THE REST OF THE CLASS FALL SILENT AND WATCH ALEX AND 001 APPROACH RESHMA AND LOUISE. THE TWO GIRLS BURST INTO AN EXPLOSION OF GIGGLES AND SIT CLOSER TOGETHER.)

RESHMA
But, Mr Simms, why have we got to work with them?

LOUISE
Yeah. It's bad enough that we've got to work with Alex, but why do we have to have the new boy as well?

MR SIMMS
Get on with your work, girls.

001
Can I sit here, please?

(ACTION – HE POINTS AT THE SPACE NEXT TO RESHMA. SHE IGNORES HIM. ALEX SITS NEXT TO LOUISE, WHO MOVES AWAY FROM HIM, CLOSER TO RESHMA.)

LOUISE
Hey, Alex, have you got any ideas about how we could improve the story?

ALEX
Well, we could …

(ACTION – THE TWO GIRLS BEGIN LAUGHING.)

RESHMA
Only joking, Alex. Why would we want your ideas?

(ACTION – 002 SIDLES OVER TO 001.)

002
I can't see any bullying here. There's been no hitting or name calling.

001
Can't you see, 002? These bullies are clever, very clever. I've spotted three already!

SONG: IT MIGHT BE A LOOK (Original)

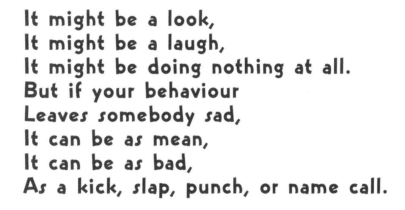

It might be a look,
It might be a laugh,
It might be doing nothing at all.
But if your behaviour
Leaves somebody sad,
It can be as mean,
It can be as bad,
As a kick, slap, punch, or name call.

(SOUND EFFECT – BELL RINGS.)

Forward to next track

Scene 3: The playground

NARRATOR
Location: Southhill School, the playground. Time: 1230 hours.

(ACTION – THE PUPILS STAND UP AND MOVE TO THEIR PLAYGROUND POSITIONS. GROUPS 002 AND 004 STAND AT THE BACK. GROUP 001 SITS AT THE FRONT. 003'S GROUP, WHICH IS THE FOCUS OF THIS SCENE, BREAKS INTO TWO. BETH AND HARRY SIT ON A BENCH AT THE BACK CHATTING TO 003, WHO IS STANDING. TOM, JACK AND RAHIM KICK A FOOTBALL AROUND IN THE MIDDLE. TOM KICKS THE BALL HARD AND IT HITS 003, WHO PICKS IT UP AND RUBS HER INJURY. THE REST OF THE CHILDREN SIT DOWN AND WATCH THE SCENE DEVELOP.)

TOM
Hey, new girl! Watch it. That ball's new!

BETH
Uh-oh. Here comes trouble …

JACK
Give us our ball back!

003
Here, sorry.

(ACTION – 003 THROWS THE BALL BACK. TOM SNATCHES IT AND COMES TO STAND RIGHT IN FRONT OF 003. HE STARES INTO HER FACE. HARRY PUSHES BETWEEN THEM, FACING TOM.)

HARRY
You just hit her with your ball and you haven't even said sorry.

TOM
(IMITATING HARRY.)
You haven't even said sorry!

BETH
Leave us alone.

RAHIM
Yeah, leave them alone, Tom. Come on. It's nearly time for lunch.

(ACTION – THE STUDENTS FREEZE IN POSITIONS THAT INDICATE PLAYING AND CHATTING. THE FOUR AGENTS HUDDLE IN A GROUP AT THE FRONT.)

002
I see what you mean, 001. There is bullying here.

004
But the good news is, there are already some other secret agents trying to stop it. Did you see Harry, Beth and Rahim?

001
This school just needs a few more people like them, then all this bullying will start to disappear.

Scene 4: The lunch queue

NARRATOR
Location: Southhill School, the lunch queue. Time: 1300 hours.

(ACTION – STUDENTS FORM A QUEUE.)

JIBRIL
(TO THE STUDENT STANDING IN FRONT OF HIM.)
Move! I don't want to stand next to you.

Script – OPERATION BULLY   CLASS ASSEMBLIES © 2010 A&C Black Publishers Ltd

CRYSTAL
(LOUDLY, TO JIBRIL.)
You can't tell me what to do. I'm staying right here.

CHLOE
(TO MEGAN, WHO IS STANDING IN FRONT OF HER.)
I'm telling everyone that you've got nits.

ELLIOT
(WHO HAS OVERHEARD.)
That's a mean thing to say. No one will believe you.

JADE
(ACTION – GIVING FRANK A BIG SHOVE.)
You trod on my new trainers!

FRANK
(FIRMLY.)
Sorry, but it was an accident. You shouldn't go around shoving people.

 SONG: WE STAND UP TOGETHER (*Sing a song of sixpence*)

Forward to next track

We stand up together
To bullying at school.
Think of others´ feelings
Is our golden rule.
If you start to bully,
Listen to us say:
Let us have a happy school
Every single day.

Scene 5: Reporting to Z

NARRATOR
Location: MI5, London. Time: 1700 hours. Keen to report on their day at Southhill School, the secret agents rush into Z's office.

(ACTION – Z IS SITTING LOOKING AT SOME PAPERS.)

001
We spotted the bullies, Ma'am.

002
It was a bit more complicated than we thought.

003

It's all to do with the way you speak and behave …

004

… whether you make people feel good or bad about themselves.

001

We didn't even need to help the students: they stood up to the bullies on their own.

Z

Well, I should have guessed you lot would need some help.

(ACTION – THE AGENTS ALL LOOK AT EACH OTHER AND COME TO A DECISION. 002 STEPS FORWARD.)

002

Actually, Ma'am, what you just said made us feel bad about ourselves.

Z

Ah … well, I'm sure it's not the same as the bullying you saw in the school. After all, you're not school children.

(ACTION – THERE IS A MOMENT'S SILENCE. THE AGENTS REFUSE TO BACK DOWN. THEY FOLD THEIR ARMS AND LOOK AT Z. SHE STARTS TO LOOK SHEEPISH.)

Z

I'm sorry. I was being rude. Anyone who stands up to bullies deserves a very special thank you.

(ACTION – Z STANDS UP AND SHAKES EACH AGENT BY THE HAND. SHE THEN MOVES TO THE MAIN STAGE AND BECKONS BETH, HARRY, RAHIM, CRYSTAL, ELLIOT AND FRANK TO THE FRONT FOR APPLAUSE.)

REPEAT SONG: WE STAND UP TOGETHER

We stand up together …

Script – OPERATION BULLY

Performance Notes

☼ Staging and performance tips (see stage plan)

- The MI5 Headquarters are on a raised platform to the right of the main stage area. The main stage serves as the school building and the playground. During each bullying incident, the other pupils stay still and watch.

- The school children are divided into four groups named after the four agents. The groups stay together when they move to new positions in the scene changes:

  001's group: Louise, Reshma, Alex.
  002's group: Jibril, Crystal, Megan, Chloe, Elliot.
  003's group: Beth, Harry, Tom, Jack, Rahim.
  004's group: Jade, Frank and the remaining school children.

- **Scene 1:** as the agents put on their disguises, the pupils start chatting and moving around the playground. When the bell rings, the pupils turn to face their teacher and sit down.

- **Scene 4:** the pupils in 002 and 004's groups line up diagonally across the stage. The pupils in 001 and 003's groups move to the back and sit down, one on the right and one on the left. The four agents remain front left.

- **Scene 5:** the agents join the rest of the cast on stage for the final song.

☼ Scenery

- Backdrop showing a school building with a playground in front of it.

☼ Props

- **MI5 headquarters:** a chair, packet of biscuits, magazine, document marked 'Top Secret', rucksack.
- **School:** four literacy exercise books, small football.

☼ Costumes

- **Agents:** long raincoats over school uniform, sun glasses.
- **Mr Simms and Z:** shirt, tie and trousers/skirt.
- **Students:** school uniform. Jade wears new trainers.

☼ Sound effects

- Mr Simms can ring the school bell (use a hand bell).

Curriculum Links

Literacy Link
Adventure and mystery.

PSHE

- The four agents thought bullying was to do with hitting, punching and name-calling, but they soon found out that bullying can be hard to spot. Encourage the children, without naming names, to relate the incidences of bullying in the story to their own experiences.

The literacy lesson

- When Agent 001 asked Reshma if he could sit next to her, what did Reshma do? How do you think 001 felt? How do you think Alex felt when Louise said, 'Why would we want your ideas?'

- Body language can be hurtful. Describe the body language in this scene.

The playground

- Talk about the way Tom and Jack spoke to Agent 003. Why is it upsetting when someone imitates your voice in a mean way?

- Which children stood up to the bullies in this scene? How did they do it?

Adults

- Look at the words spoken by Mr Simms and Z. Ask for volunteers to speak them in the way they imagine the characters would have said them. Would you like Mr Simms as your teacher or Z as your boss?

New pupils

- Tom said, 'Hey, new girl! Watch it.' Was this a nice way to treat a new pupil? Invite any pupils who have recently joined the class to talk about their first few days at school. What was good and what was not so good?

Drama

- Act out the bullying scenes in the play. Follow each one up with a courteous version.

Art and design

- Make a backdrop depicting your own school. First, make sketches of the exterior of the building from different angles. Discuss its age and condition, the type and colour of the materials used, etc. Choose one aspect of the building and sketch it on the backdrop. Fill in the building outline using sponge rollers – experiment to find shades of colour that match your bricks and roof tiles.

Year of the Rat by Veronica Clark

Cast
Main narrator
Animal narrators (12)
The animals – Rat, Snake, Monkey, Tiger, Ox, Pig, Dog, Rabbit, Ram, Horse, Rooster, Dragon (12)
Emperor
Princess
River dancers (2 or 4)

The twelve animal narrators double up as race commentators.

Assembly theme
Year of the Rat is about leadership, with a focus on the qualities required to be a good leader. It also touches on democratic decision-making.

Story
This play is based on a well-known Chinese legend, describing how Rat becomes the leader of the animals for the coming new year. The animals lie dozing in the sunshine, but this peaceful idyll is shattered when Dragon enters and declares that from this day onwards, each new year will be named after him. The animals are enraged by the presumption of Dragon and proceed, in turn, to say why he or she is best suited for the role.

Things are getting heated, when the Princess, sent by her father, the Emperor, comes down from her hilltop palace to see what's going on. The Princess suggests that the quarrel be settled by having a swimming competition: the first across the river will be the new leader.

Rat, who is determined to win at any cost, jumps onto Ox's back and is the first to set foot on the opposite river bank. The animals are cross with Rat because he cheated, but the Princess defuses the situation by declaring that, because all the animals have good leadership qualities, they shall take it in turn to be leaders.

Setting
The setting is a riverbank in rural China.

Songs
The three songs are set to original tunes. The first, *Song of the river*, could be sung as a solo.

Script: Year of the Rat

Scene 1: On the river bank

SONG: SONG OF THE RIVER (*Original*)

Sun in the sky,
Tall swaying trees,
River flows on to the sea.
On and on, and on and on, to the distant sea.

Mountains up high,
Scent on the breeze,
River flows on to the sea.
On and on, and on and on, to the distant sea.

Forward to next track

MAIN NARRATOR
Let's meet the twelve animals in our Chinese New Year story. One of them is a dragon – but we'll leave him until last.

RAT'S NARRATOR (1)
Can you see Rat? He's over there on the riverbank, admiring his reflection and dangling his long tail in the water. He's a charming fellow.
(ACTION – RAT HUMS.)

SNAKE'S NARRATOR (2)
Snake's almost hidden in the long grass. She's a big thinker, is Snake.
(ACTION – SNAKE HISSES.)

MONKEY'S NARRATOR (3)
There's Monkey, high up in his tree, weaving leaves together. He's always making things. (ACTION – MONKEY SCRATCHES.)

TIGER'S NARRATOR (4)
It's hard to spot Tiger, because of her stripes. She's probably asleep in the long grass, dreaming about winning a fight. (ACTION – TIGER SNARLS.)

OX'S NARRATOR (5)
Here's Ox, on his way down to the river to drink – same time, same place, every day. Always dependable. (ACTION – OX SLURPS.)

PIG'S NARRATOR (6)

You can't miss Pig – she's over there in the mud. She's a mine of information. (ACTION – PIG GRUNTS.)

DOG'S NARRATOR (7)

Dog's a loyal creature, but a bit snappy. He just won't leave Rabbit alone. (ACTION – DOG BARKS AT RABBIT.)

RABBIT'S NARRATOR (8)

As you can see, Rabbit isn't too worried by Dog – mind you, she's had a few lucky escapes. (ACTION – RABBIT THUMPS FOOT.)

RAM'S NARRATOR (9)

Ram is at the back, admiring the view. He has quite an eye for beauty. (ACTION – RAM GAZES AROUND DREAMILY.)

HORSE'S NARRATOR (10)

Horse is clever – no denying that. What she doesn't know about grass isn't worth knowing! (ACTION – HORSE GRAZES.)

ROOSTER'S NARRATOR (11)

Where's Rooster? He's usually hard at work somewhere. Ah, there he is. He looks a bit flustered! (ACTION – ROOSTER FLUTTERS ON STAGE.)

ROOSTER

Cock-a-doodle-doo. Cock-a-doodle-doo.
Here comes Dragon. Cock-a-doodle-SHOO!
(ACTION – ROOSTER SHOOS THE ANIMALS AWAY TO MAKE ROOM FOR DRAGON.)

DRAGON'S NARRATOR (12)

Trust Dragon to make an entrance. He has a very high opinion of himself. (ACTION – DRAGON STALKS ON, RATTLING HIS SCALES. HE STANDS ON THE LOW STAGE BLOCK IN THE MIDDLE OF THE STAGE AND GAZES AROUND HAUGHTILY.)

Scene 2: The argument

DRAGON

(CLEARING HIS THROAT.)
We need to talk.

MAIN NARRATOR

The eleven animals look expectantly at Dragon.

DRAGON

I've decided that from now on, I'm going to be your leader. Every year will be named after me: the Year of the Dragon.

MAIN NARRATOR

There is a moment of shocked silence, then, one by one, the animals speak.

RAT

But I'm so charming, I should be the new leader.

SNAKE

But I'm so wise and beautiful, I should be the new leader.

MONKEY

But I am so creative, I should be the new leader.

TIGER

But I am so brave, I should be the new leader.

OX

But I am so calm and dependable, I should be the new leader.

PIG

But I am so learned, I should be the new leader.

DOG

But I am so loyal, I should be the new leader.

RABBIT

But I am so lucky, I should be the new leader.

RAM

But I am so artistic, I should be the new leader.

HORSE

But I am so clever, I should be the new leader.

ROOSTER

But I am so hard-working, I should be the new leader.

MAIN NARRATOR

Dragon is quite taken aback. He is so strong and fierce that he hadn't expected the other animals to question his leadership.

 Script – YEAR OF THE RAT

The animals' discussion gets more and more heated, and they begin to shout and jump around. (ACTION AND SOUND EFFECTS – HISSES, GRUNTS, BARKS, BELLOWS, SNARLS ETC.)

Tiger takes a swipe at Dog, and Pig thrusts her snout in Ox's face. (ACTION.)

Rat, who is well-known for his hot temper, jumps up and down on the spot, punching the air. (ACTION.)

Only Rabbit keeps quiet – she goes into a deep sulk. (ACTION – RABBIT GOES OFF TO THE BACK OF THE STAGE AND SULKS.)

(CD) 52/60

SONG: **WHO WILL BE THE LEADER?** (Original)

Squeak, hiss, chatter and roar.
Who will be the leader for the brand new year?
Grunt, bark, bleat and neigh.
Who will be the leader this year?

Me, me, me, me, me.
I will be the leader for the brand new year.
Me, me, me, me, me.
I will be the leader this year.

Squeak, hiss, chatter and roar.
Who will be the leader for the brand new year?
Grunt, bark, bleat and neigh.
Who will be the leader this year?

Forward to next track

Scene 3: The Princess

MAIN NARRATOR
Up in his mountain palace, the Emperor hears the quarrelling, and he sends his daughter down to find out what is going on.
(ACTION – PRINCESS MOVES FROM THE MOUNTAIN PALACE TO THE RIVER.)

When the animals see the Princess approaching, they stop shouting and bow down before her. (ACTION – ANIMALS BOW.)

The Princess looks around at the hot, angry animals and says:

PRINCESS
My word. You do look upset. What's the matter?

DRAGON
The years should be named after me because I would be the best leader.

The other animals start quietly hissing and muttering and chattering and twitching. (ACTION AND ANIMAL SOUNDS.)

The Princess realises that something has to be done before full-scale animal war breaks out. Holding up her hand (ACTION), she says:

PRINCESS
Stop! Stop! I have an idea.

MAIN NARRATOR
The animals stop their quarrelling and look at her.

PRINCESS
We shall have a swimming race across the river. The New Year will be named after the winner.

MAIN NARRATOR
Dog, who likes justice to be done (and is a good swimmer), says:

DOG
Good idea. Line up everyone.

MAIN NARRATOR
The animals spread out along the riverbank. The Princess calls out:

PRINCESS
READY, STEADY, GO!

Scene 4: The race

NARRATORS

1 Into the water spring the animals. (ACTION – ANIMALS MIME SWIMMING.)

2 They're making a terrific splash. (SOUND EFFECTS – SPLASHING.)

3 At this stage of the race, it's hard to see who is in the lead.

CHANT: THEY'RE OFF (Original)

They're off, they're off,
To the other side of the river.
They're off, they're off,
With a splishetty, splashetty splosh.

NARRATORS

4 Tiger is in the lead! Yes, Tiger is definitely in the lead.

5 Monkey is making a big splash, but isn't getting very far.

6 Rooster has given up!

REPEAT CHANT: THEY'RE OFF

They're off, they're off ...

NARRATORS

7 Horse is putting on a spurt ... Her tail has got tangled in Ram's horns!

8 Oh no! Rabbit is panicking and trying to climb onto Snake's back.

9 Rat is swimming very close to Ox – I think they are going to collide!

REPEAT CHANT: THEY'RE OFF

They're off, they're off ...

NARRATORS

10 Ox has taken the lead.

11 Steam is pouring out of Dragon's nostrils. He just can't overtake Ox.

12 Rat looks tired, but he's still sticking close to Ox.

SONG: A CUNNING PLAN (*Bobby Shafto*)

How can I win this swimming race?
How can I win this swimming race?
How can I win this swimming race?
I want to be the leader!

Ah ha! I have a cunning plan,
Ah ha! I have a cunning plan,
Ah ha! I have a cunning plan,
I will become the leader!

MAIN NARRATOR

Ox doesn't notice Rat climb onto his back. Just before he reaches the opposite side of the river, Rat runs along his nose, leaps onto the bank and shouts triumphantly:

RAT
I AM THE WINNER!

Scene 5: The Year of the Rat

MAIN NARRATOR
The rest of the animals clamber out of the water, looking tired and dejected. (ACTION – THE ANIMALS CRAWL OUT OF THE RIVER.)

Ox is very cross with Rat.
(ACTION – OX POINTS AT RAT AND SHAKES HIS HEAD.)

The Princess feels sorry for the animals because they have all tried so hard.

She thinks hard for a few moments. Then she smiles and says:

PRINCESS
I have an idea. This New Year will be named after Rat. But the next eleven years will be named after each of you in turn. I think you will all make good leaders.

MAIN NARRATOR
The animals think that this is a very good idea. They nod and then shake hands with each other.
(ACTION – ANIMALS SHAKE HANDS, ALTHOUGH NOT WITH RAT.)

Then, one by one they go back to their homes to dry out.
(ACTION – ANIMALS WALK BACK TO THEIR STARTING POSITIONS.)

Rat stays where he is. He does a little victory dance before lying on a rock to make plans for the New Year.
(ACTION – RAT DANCES.)

 REPEAT SONG: SONG OF THE RIVER

 Sun in the sky ...

Script – YEAR OF THE RAT

Performance Notes

Staging and performance tips (see stage plans)

- The twelve race commentators play a significant part in this drama and should be visible throughout. They should stand (in the order they speak) on benches. Either place the benches on each side of the stage, or behind the main stage area. The twelve animals begin at the back of the stage, then swim across the river in the middle to the front of the stage. Finally, they return to their starting places by walking round to either the left or right of the stage. Put markers on the floor to help the animal actors to remember their places.

- **Scene 1**: at the start of the play, all the animals except Ox, Rooster and Dragon are on stage. During *Song of the river*, the dancers carry their drape onto the stage and lay it across the middle, from right to left. They gently shake it to give the impression of moving water. When Ox is introduced, he enters on the right and lumbers across to lie on Rat's left. Rooster flutters on from the left to warn the animals Dragon is approaching. He is followed by Dragon, who strikes a pose on the low stage block positioned centre back.

- **Scene 2**: one at a time, the animals stand to put forwards their case for leadership, then sit down again.

- **Scene 3**: the Princess stays on the raised block all the time she is on stage. Ox and Rat should be next to each other when the animals line up along the side of the river for the race.

- **Scene 4**: the Princess starts the race, and the animals lie down on the drape and quietly paddle around as though swimming (not too vigorously). Everyone except the animals joins in the repeated chant *They're off*. Apart from Rooster, who gives up and returns to his starting place, the animals don't do the things described by the race commentators. Towards the end of the race, Rat stands to sing *A cunning plan*. He then stands with his legs on either side of Ox's back, jumps out on the opposite bank and declares himself the winner. The river dancers need to keep a firm grip of the drape during the race.

- **Scene 5**: on their way back to their starting places, the animals don't cross the river again; instead they crawl and creep off the stage on the right or left (depending which side they are on), past the river dancers and back on stage at the back.

☼ Scenery

- **Mountain palace:** cover a tall piece of PE equipment with a purple drape. Fix silver or grey rocks to the fabric. Provide a step halfway up the mountain for the Princess to stand on. The Emperor sits cross-legged on top of the mountain throughout the play. Suspend a few large clouds from the ceiling above the mountain.

- **Willow trees:** attach long, thin, curled strips of green paper to strong one-dimensional card trunks. They should hang almost to the ground. Keep the trees upright by fastening them to freestanding PE equipment.

☼ Costumes

- **Narrators/race commentators:** black trousers, long-sleeved black or white tops and plimsolls. They could wear trilby hats when commenting on the race.

- **Animals:** tights or trousers and plain, long-sleeved tops in appropriate colours. Dress Snake, Rooster and Dragon in bright colours. Sew stripes of black felt on Tiger's costume, and shiny green spots on Snake's top. Dress Rooster in a short, full, black skirt, and make wings out of a black plastic bag decorated with coloured felt feathers. Use rope, fur fabric, wool or stuffed tights for tails. Dragon can wear a shiny gold or red cloak.

- Use face paints for whiskers, noses and stripes, and make headbands for those animals with beaks, ears and/or horns.

- **Emperor and Princess:** long, Chinese-style dressing gowns over black trousers and t-shirts. Give the Emperor a drooping moustache. The Princess can wear a wide sash and Chinese-style hair decorations, and carry a fan.

- **River dancers:** blue or green tights, and long-sleeved tops with strips of blue, silver and green plastic or fabric attached.

☼ Sound effects

- In Scene 1, with the exception of Monkey's scratching (light maraca), Horse's grazing (guiro), Rooster's fluttering (quiet jingles) and Dragon's scale rattling (clappers), the animals make their own vocal sound effects – barking, grunting etc. A few race narrators can shake tambourines to make splashing sounds during the race across the river.

Curriculum Links

Literacy Link
Stories from a range of cultures.

PSHE

Leadership

- At the start of the play, the animals described one aspect of their characters that, in their opinion, made them eligible for the role of leader. Make a list of these qualities and ask the children which of them are relevant to good leadership and why. Do you think Dragon would have made a good leader? Did Rat deserve to be the leader? Was the swimming race a good way to choose the new leader?

> **ACTIVITY BOX: WHO WILL BE THE LEADER?**
> Find twelve volunteers to represent the animals. Ask them to make short speeches describing what they are good at, and why this quality makes them eligible for the role of leader for the new year. Follow this up with a secret ballot. The teacher counts the votes and declares the winner. Next time there is a class conflict or problem to solve, if appropriate, ask the elected leader to suggest how to go about it.

- Ask the children to identify some of the good leadership qualities possessed by other children in the class. Give examples of how these qualities improve class life.

History

Leaders
- Find out about some great leaders of the past. What did they achieve? Who do you think is great living leader?

Geography

Rivers
- Discuss rivers with the class. Where do they start and where do they usually end up? Name some of the most famous rivers in the world and find them on maps. Which is the longest river in the world?

☼ Stage Plans

✦ GOING FOR GOALS ✦

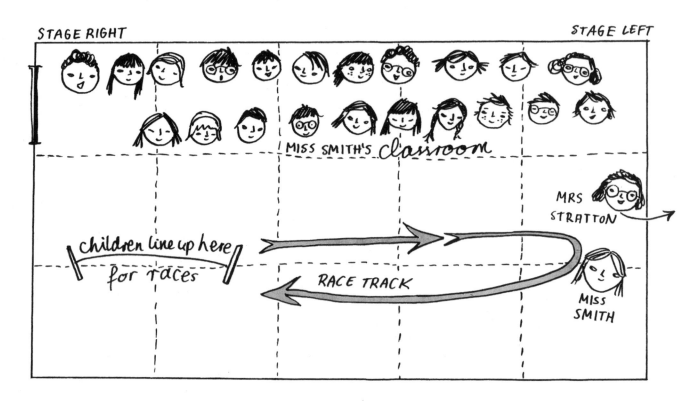

~ ROBIN HOOD ~

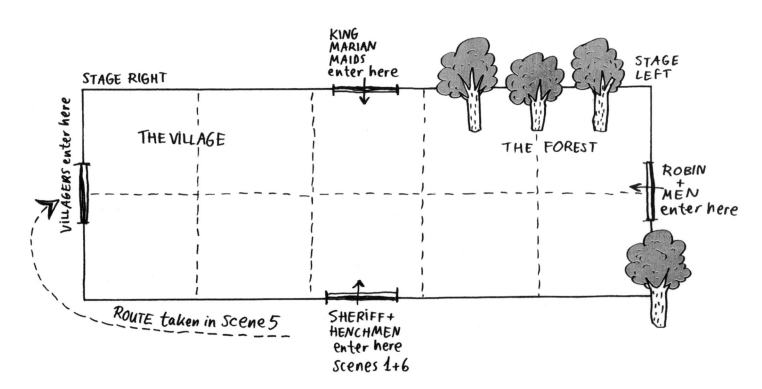

→ OPERATION BULLY ←

MI5 HEADQUARTERS

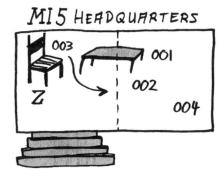

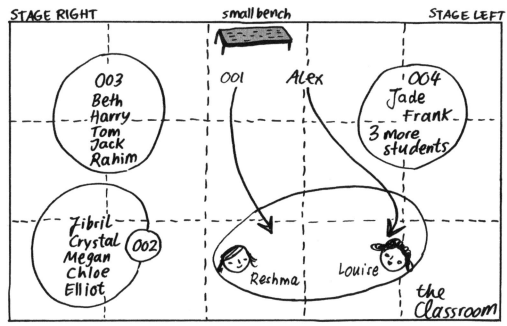

STAGE RIGHT   small bench   STAGE LEFT

003
Beth
Harry
Tom
Jack
Rahim

001   Alex

004
Jade
Frank
3 more students

Jibril
Crystal
Megan
Chloe
Elliot

002

Reshma   Louise

the Classroom

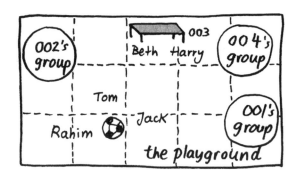

002's group

003 Beth Harry

004's group

Tom

Jack

Rahim

001's group

the playground

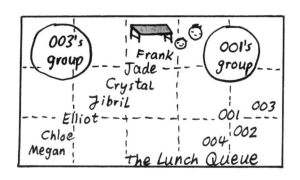

003's group

Frank
Jade
Crystal
Jibril
Elliot
Chloe
Megan

001's group

003
001
004 002

The Lunch Queue

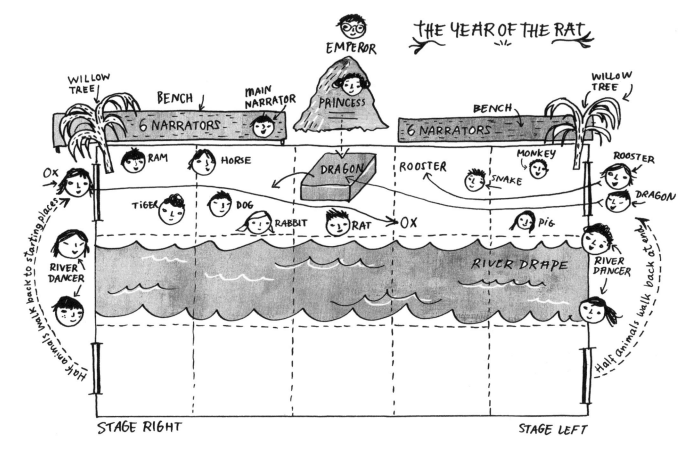

THE YEAR OF THE RAT

SEAL Links

Going for goals

Going for goals
I can foresee obstacles and plan to overcome them when I am setting goals.
The three children knew that they might be worried on the actual day of the timed races, but also knew their teacher and classmates would be supporting them.
I can recognise when I have reached my goal.
The children were proud of themselves for overcoming their worries and taking part in the races.

Robin Hood

New beginnings
I understand why we need to have different rules in different places.
Robin had one set of rules for himself and his men, and wanted a fair set of laws for his countrymen that would remove the need for him to act in an apparently lawless way.

Say no to bullying
I can tell you why witnesses sometimes join in with bullying or don't tell.
Perhaps the henchmen went along with the Sheriff's bullying because they'd be punished if they didn't.

Operation Bully

Say no to bullying
I can tell you what bullying is.
By the end of the play, the agents had a good idea of what bullying is.
I know how it might feel to be a witness to and the target of bullying.
The students who stuck up for the people being bullied empathised with the victims.

Getting on and falling out
I can use peaceful problem solving to sort out difficulties.
The agents and students stood up to the bullies in a peaceful way.

Year of the Rat

New beginnings
I can tell you one special thing about me.
Each animal recounted something special about him/herself.

Getting on and falling out
I can use peaceful problem-solving to sort out difficulties.
The Princess stopped the animals from fighting, and helped them to find a peaceful way to decide who was to become the new leader.

Melody Lines

Going for Goals

Tick, tock, tick

Miss Smith had a watch That she hard-ly ev-er used, So she did-n't know the time or the date._____ Miss Smith had a watch That she hard-ly ev-er used, So she kept miss-ing things and be-ing late._____ Les-sons went on too long, Tick, tock, tick, tock. Tea-cher got it all wrong, Tick, tock, tick! Miss

Silly Billy/Sensible Billy

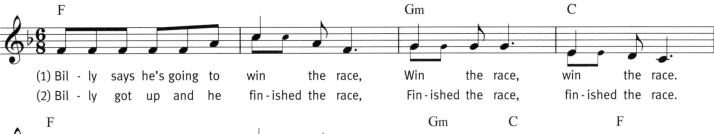

(1) Bil-ly says he's going to win the race, Win the race, win the race.
(2) Bil-ly got up and he fin-ished the race, Fin-ished the race, fin-ished the race.

Bil-ly says he's going to win the race, With-out the help of his friends.
Bil-ly got up and he fin-ished the race, With just a bit____ of help.

Robin Hood

Bold, brave Robin

Gon-na tell you all a sto-ry, And we hope you find it good. It's the sto-ry of an out-law, With the name of Ro-bin Hood. He__ lived in Sher-wood For-est, Where he built a se-cret den. And he had some bold ad-ven-tures, With his band of mer-ry men. Bold, brave Ro-bin! We'd like to shake your hand. Three cheers for no-ble Ro-bin, Who brought jus-tice to the land.

So bad

The She-riff is nas-ty and greed-y,____ He fills all our hearts with dis-may.____ He tax-es the poor and the need-y,____ And takes all our mo-ney a-way.____ So bad, so sad, To take all our mo-ney a-way, a-way. So bad, so sad, To take all our mo-ney a-way.____

Melody Lines – ROBIN HOOD

We're the Merry Men

We're the Mer-ry Men, the ve - ry Mer-ry Men, We laugh and sing like a - ny - thing, 'Cos we're the Mer-ry Men! We live in the wood, help - ing Ro - bin Hood, We hang out in our se - cret den, 'Cos we're the Mer - ry Men.

Justice for all

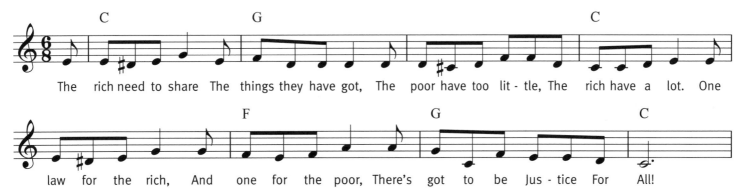

The rich need to share The things they have got, The poor have too lit - tle, The rich have a lot. One law for the rich, And one for the poor, There's got to be Jus - tice For All!

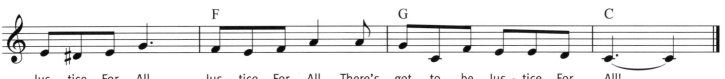

Jus - tice For All, Jus - tice For All, The poor and the weak, The meek and the small. Jus - tice For All, Jus - tice For All, There's got to be Jus - tice For All!_____

Operation Bully

How can we spot a bully?

How can we spot a bul-ly? How can we spot a bul-ly? Do they slap and kick and punch like this?
How can we spot a bul-ly? How can we spot a bul-ly? Do they call you names to your face?

Slap and kick and punch like this? Slap and kick and punch like this? Let's find that bul-ly.
Call you names to your face? Call you names to your face? Let's find that bul-ly.

It might be a look

It might be a look, It might be a laugh, It might be do-ing no-thing at all.__

__ But if your be-ha-viour leaves some-bo-dy sad,__ It can be as mean, It

can be as bad,__ As a kick, slap, punch, or name call.

We stand up together

We stand up to-ge-ther To bul-ly-ing at school. Think of o-thers' feel-ings Is our gold-en rule.

If you start to bul-ly, Lis-ten to us say: Let us have a hap-py school Ev-'ry sin-gle day.

Year of the Rat

Song of the river

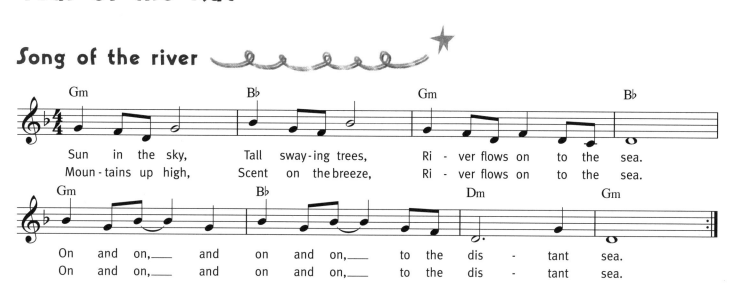

Sun in the sky, Tall sway-ing trees, Ri - ver flows on to the sea.
Moun-tains up high, Scent on the breeze, Ri - ver flows on to the sea.

On and on,___ and on and on,___ to the dis - tant sea.
On and on,___ and on and on,___ to the dis - tant sea.

Who will be the leader?

Squeak, hiss, chat-ter and roar. Who will be the lea-der for the brand new year?
Me, me, me, me, me. I will be the lea-der for the brand new year.

Grunt, bark, bleat and neigh. Who will be the lea-der this year?
Me, me, me, me, me. I will be the lea-der this year.

A cunning plan

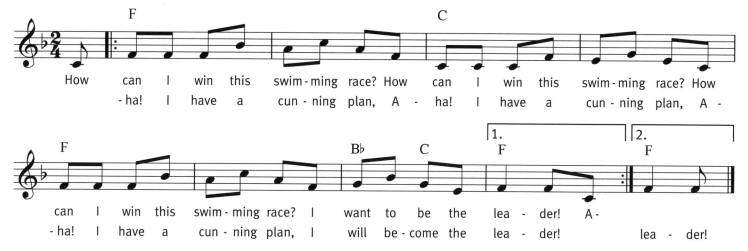

How can I win this swim-ming race? How can I win this swim-ming race? How
- ha! I have a cun-ning plan, A - ha! I have a cun-ning plan, A -

can I win this swim-ming race? I want to be the lea - der! A -
- ha! I have a cun-ning plan, I will be - come the lea - der! lea - der!

And finally ...

Performance licence information

To present an informal performance of any of the class assemblies from this publication, you do not need to purchase a separate performance licence. An informal performance is a performance, with or without an audience, that takes place within an educational establishment or church, where box office takings are less than £250.

You may also make copies of the audio CD solely for the purpose of preparing for and aiding an informal performance within the establishment for which the original script was purchased without paying a further fee. Any copies made must not be distributed outside of the establishment for which the original script was purchased, and must be destroyed once the performance has taken place. Any other copying is strictly prohibited.

If you wish to video or record a performance, either for your own internal use or in order to sell copies to parents, you must write to us separately to obtain permission. See below for our contact details.

If you wish to present a performance of any of the class assemblies from this publication where any box office takings will exceed £250, you must contact us for permission and an appropriate performance licence:
The Copyright Manager
Music Department
A&C Black Publishers Ltd
36 Soho Square
London W1D 3QY
music@acblack.com

About the authors

Veronica Clark is author of *High Low Dolly Pepper* (A&C Black), the Christmas musical *The Raggedy King* (Starshine Music), and co-author of *Three Little Nativities* and *Three Little Celebrations* (A&C Black). She was music advisor to BBC WATCH programme, *The Song Catcher*, and is a former primary headteacher and specialist in music education for pre-school and infant children. She believes that involving young children in musicals provides them with an exciting and relevant educational experience, which encourages them to experience all areas of the curriculum.

Kaye Umansky taught for fourteen years in London primary schools, specialising in drama and music. She has been a full-time children's author for the last twenty-five years and has written many plays, music books and novels, including the *Pongwiffy* series (Bloomsbury), *Three Tapping Teddies*, *Three Singing Pigs*, *Three Rocking Crocs*, and the award-winning *Three Rapping Rats* (A&C Black), and is also co-author of *Three Little Nativities* and *Three Little Celebrations* (A&C Black). She lives in London with her husband, daughter and two cats.

Pippa Goodhart went from bookselling into writing, and has had over seventy children's books published since then, ranging from picture books, through early readers to novels. Her picture book *You Choose* has sold three quarters of a million copies, and is one of Bookstart's chosen books for three year-olds. Her novels have been shortlisted for six major awards. She also writes as Laura Owen when writing the *Winnie the Witch* stories. She combines writing with teaching both children and adults.

Jenny McLachlan is an Advanced Skills English teacher who works in East Sussex. She has written stories for children and teenagers and has created a wide range of English teaching resources. Through her work, she is involved in educational research and promoting good teaching practice in primary and secondary schools. She has a passion for children's literature and a belief that it is through engaging with imaginative writing that children learn about their world.

Acknowledgements

Story of *Going for Goals* © 2010 Pippa Goodhart
Songs: *Silly Billy* and *Sensible Billy*, words © Pippa Goodhart, music traditional
Tick, tock, tick, words and music © Veronica Clark
Give it a go! and *We gave it a go!* words © Pippa Goodhart
My goal, words © Veronica Clark
Story of *Robin Hood* © 2010 Kaye Umansky
Songs: *Bold, brave Robin*, *So bad* and *We're the Merry Men*, words © Kaye Umansky, music traditional
Justice for all, words and music © Kaye Umansky
Story of *Operation Bully* © 2010 Jenny McLachlan
Songs: *We stand up together*, words © Jenny McLachlan, music traditional
How can we spot a bully and *It might be a look*, words © Jenny McLachlan, music © Jenny McLachlan and Veronica Clark
Story of *Year of the rat* © 2010 Veronica Clark
Songs: *A cunning plan*, words © Veronica Clark, music traditional
Song of the river and *Who will be the leader*, words and music © Veronica Clark
They're off! words © Veronica Clark

Teaching activities © 2010 Veronica Clark

Cover illustration © 2010 Tim Hopgood
Cover design by Jane Tetzlaff and Sara Oiestad
Inside illustrations © 2010 Christiane Engel
Edited by Lucy Mitchell
Text design by Fiona Grant
Music setting by Jeanne Roberts
Recorded arrangements, incidental music, sound engineering and mastering by Matthew Moore
Songs sung by Kaz Simmons

The publishers and authors would like to thank the following people:
Ocklynge Junior School
Year 3: Alan Shuttleworth, Kate Whitburn and pupils in 3WP, Julie Nightingale and pupils in 3NS, Gemma Burke and pupils in 3B, Jane Morrish and pupils in 3M.
Shinewater County Primary
Moira Smith-Nicholls.

First published 2010
A&C Black
36 Soho Square, London W1D 3QY
© 2010 A&C Black
ISBN: 978-1-4081-2458-1
Printed in Great Britain by Caligraving Ltd, Thetford, Norfolk